~ Lust and Lace ~

a Victorian Romance and Erotic Short Story
Collection.

Vol. I

by
Lady T. L. Jennings

My Secret Quill

~ Lust and Lace ~

a Victorian Romance and Erotic Short Story Collection.

Vol. I

First edition.

First published in United Kingdom by My Secret Quill, 2016.

ISBN: 9781520120133

www.mysecretquill.com

Also by Lady T. L. Jennings

*

Gay Victorian Romance and Erotica

~ Different Desire ~
a Gay Victorian Romance and Erotic Novelette
Collection. Vol. I.

~ Forbidden Feelings ~
a Gay Victorian Romance and Erotic Novelette
Collection. Vol. II.

~ Complicated Affairs ~
a Gay Victorian Romance and Erotic Novella

~ Blackmail ~
a Gay Victorian Romance and Erotic Novella

~ The Mystery of the Black Widow ~
a Gay Victorian Romance and Erotic Novella

~ A Thief in the Night ~
a Gay Victorian Romance and Erotic Novella

*

~ Lust and Lace ~

a Victorian Romance and Erotic
short story collection.
Vol. I.

Short stories:
St Hubert's Day Fox Hunting
Strange Masks
View of a cemetery
Master and Servant
Booklover
The Portrait of Mrs Elliott
Wildflowers
The Governess

* * *

~ St Hubert's Day Fox Hunting ~

"I hate that stupid horse! And I hate this stupid bloody hunt, as well!"

Quentin had always detested the yearly St Hubert's Day Fox Hunting. First of all, the English weather in November was usually cold and damp; and secondly, Quentin was not at all fond of riding around like a madman hunting a fox in the middle of nowhere, when instead he could be sitting in front of the fire in his study with a nice book and a cup of tea.

But oh no, his father demanded that his oldest son had to compete in the big hunt, no matter what the weather was like, so here he was, on a deserted and muddy road just a couple of hours before sundown. The horse had taken off rapidly after leaving him swearing loudly in a thorny bush, and now he had to walk all the way home to the estate, wet and soggy, just to be greeted by his father and brothers' humiliating glares and questions. And all he wanted was to sit by the fire with a cup of tea and a book.

Quentin continued to walk down the country road while his riding boots slowly filled up with water from the endless rain. His father had arranged the foxhunting for more than twenty years on the property, a tradition that had started in 1840. This was the fifth time Quentin participated and he had never won or killed a fox yet.

He had, however, lost his riding bowler and his black hair ribbon, so his blonde wet hair was plastered to his head by the rain. After an hour of vowing that he would never ever celebrate St Hubert's Day again, with or without hunting, he came to the horrible conclusion that not only was he wet and cold, he was also hopelessly lost.

His father's property was large, the third largest in whole Devon, a fact his father liked to point out at their dinner parties; and the property was filled with old fields and forest crossed by even older country roads. Farming had ended decades ago and the land was used mostly for hunting and occasionally logging of the large oak trees that grew in the area.

Therefore it was quite possible to walk for hours without meeting a soul to ask for directions, as Quentin now gloomily found out. Every now and then he stopped to listen for the hunters' horns or the barking of their dogs, but all he heard was the light pouring of the rain and the sound of his teeth clattering together due to the cold and his shivers.

*

As dusk crept forward over the forest, Quentin realised that no one was going to find him and that the search party, which probably was out there looking for him, had to stop for the night. The best thing he could do was to find shelter, if he would stand any chance of surviving the night. Quentin continued forward along the road, scanning the forest and the overgrown fields for an old farmer's house or hunting cabin, but found none. He had almost given up hope now and started to look for a fallen tree or a small animal cave, which could provide at least some protection from the rain. A slight breeze made the few leaves that were left on the trees whisper in the wind.

Suddenly he saw a small light ahead in the dark. First he thought it was a trick of the light, but there it was again: A small firelight of some kind to the left of the road.

Maybe it is a lantern or a torch? Quentin thought and followed the light, which gave him a small flicker of hope in the now completely dark forest. Quentin staggered forward, not losing the light with his eyes, even when he fell several times over stones and branches on the old country road.

At last he stood in front of a little cabin, no more than a shack. The light came indeed from a lantern and it swayed gently from its old rusty chain in the wind.

"Hello? Is there anyone in there? Open immediately, for the love of God!" Quentin cried out and banged weakly on the shabby wooden door.

It opened slowly, and for a moment he could not see anything else in the cottage except the blessed fire in the far corner. Without waiting for an invitation, Quentin stumbled forward to the fireplace, fell to his knees and spread his numb hands in front of the fire. He closed his eyes as the heat spread slowly from his fingers up along his arms not caring about who or what that had opened the door.

"Thank heavens for this fire and its warmth," he mumbled, and flinched when a female voice with a strange accent replied,

"Or, you could just thank me instead."

Some sense came back to Quentin, and he realised that this could very well be a trap of some sort. After all, he was the oldest son and kidnappings in Devon and Cornwall were frequently occurring. He turned around rapidly but fell; his cold legs refused to follow his quick command. The cottage was small and contained nothing more than a small bed, a wooden three-legged chair and an aged cupboard, and at first he did not notice the woman in the shadows.

"W-who are you?" he managed to say, laying half on his back in front of the fire staring at the figure in the shadows behind the still opened door.

"My name is Holly and I live here in the forest," she said as she stepped into the light and closed the door behind her.

She was dressed in rags, which once might have been a sturdy green woollen peasant dress and a brown knitted cloak, but what really caught Quentin's attention was her hair. It was red. Not

Irish red, but almost orange in the light from the fire. It was not braided or even covered, as any decent woman would have kept her hair, but instead spilled down freely over her shoulders in curls down to her waist. Strangely, even though her dress consisted of only filthy rags, her hair looked clean and dry.

"The November nights in England can be cold and easily claim a young man's life," she said. "Lucky for you that you stumbled over my cabin, eh?" she continued with a small smile, which showed that she lacked a tooth next to her front teeth. She was otherwise a pretty girl, with a heart shaped face, large dark eyes and a slim figure.

"…Yes, well, that is true," Quentin said slowly as he tried to regain his composure. "However, you do know that you are on my father's property? And he does not tolerate squatters on his lands. If I may suggest, you might consider…"

He trailed off as Holly turned her back against him and started to collect some dried herbs that hung from the cottage's ceiling. The ceiling was broken; rainclouds and the first sight of the moon could easily been seen through the broken woodwork.

The nerve! Quentin was outraged. *She had not called him "sir or My Lord", she was dressed improperly, not to mention the lack of braids or a decent head protection. And now she even turned her back against him when he talked. It was…*

His thoughts were interrupted as Holly went past him, placed a battered iron pot by the fire, and added the herbs into it by crushing them together with her thin pale fingers.

"Do not worry, Quentin," she said. "We are not in your father's forest anymore. Save your energy and worry if you want to survive this night. You are cold and full of bruises, and you need to rest. There is a bed over there. Why do you not go there and lay down while I make you some soup, eh?"

Without answering, Quentin realised that he indeed was overwhelmingly tired, and while he was not numb with cold anymore, the small bed with its mattress of hay undeniably looked inviting. He rose without a word and managed to take off his red riding jacket but forgot about the boots as he fell into oblivion on the bed.

*

Someone called his name from far away. At first he did not want to wake up, but the voice with the strange accent refused to be silent.

"Here, I have made you some soup. You need to eat something hot, or the November cold may still claim you," the woman said.

He opened his eyes. The fire had burned down but its light still illuminated her silhouette and unkempt hair. The soup was made of various vegetables and some sort of meat and tasted strongly of herbs, which left a slightly acid aftertaste. Quentin felt weak but refused to get handfed and ate the whole bowl of soup while Holly watched him. He drank cold water from a wooden mug that she gave him. It was not until after he had finished his meal and he saw his clothes, neatly folded and placed on the three-legged chair by the fire, that he became conscious over the fact that he indeed was naked under the thick blanket. Quentin blushed and was suddenly very glad over the dim light in the cabin.

"Feeling better now, eh?" she asked as he handed her the bowl and the mug. He mumbled something indistinguishable in reply, pulled the blanket up to his chin and closed his eyes, pretending to go back to sleep but keeping one eye slightly open to see what the strange woman would to next. First she fidgeted with the bowl and the mug in the corner by the cupboard, and after that she lighted a couple of small thin rods by the fireplace, where they burned slowly and left a sweet scent in the air.

Then, in the last light from the dying fire, she turned around and undressed. Under the old peasant dress she wore a loosely tied corset and a chemise, both in light colours. She had pale skin and a frail body. Frail, yes, but still delicate, with a small, rounded apple bosom with pink nipples. Her thighs were nicely shaped and her waist was thin.

Quentin's breathing grew rapid as she slowly approached the bed. He had still not known the love of a woman, a privilege that only applied to those who had entered marriage; and his few adventures with tavern girls or servants had never included even a glimpse of a leg and definitively not the sight of an uncovered breast nor a naked woman. Her heart-shaped face was framed by red hair and large brown eyes looked down at him. The bed all of a sudden felt extremely small as Holly slipped under the blanket.

She was warm and soft and whispered in his ear: "I know that you still are awake." She turned her body towards his and placed a warm hand on his beating chest.

"Who are you?" he asked quietly.

"Only a poor peasant girl," she whispered with a smile and kissed him gently. He kissed her back and soon forgot his question. He explored her tongue and lips lightly until she moved closer and pressed her naked body against his.

The kisses rapidly became more intense and once he by accident happened to bite her, which made her lip bleed a little. A slight taste of blood mingled with their kisses.

It felt as if every thought and sense of sanity left him. He could no longer feel his bruises from falling of the horse, nor did he care about his father's hunt or the bitter cold he had experienced. Instead he grew hot, burning hot under her fingers, as if her touch had woken something deep inside of him.

He pushed himself against her rhythmically and she answered with the same pace until they lay naked, panting and sweaty, with the blanket long forgotten on the cottage's dirty floor.

"What are you doing to me?" he asked, but she only smiled with her missing tooth and her hands followed down his body until they reached their goal, which made Quentin unsure if he had spoken at all.

Her fingers touched the most sensitive spot on his body and he could feel himself instantly grow harder, harder than he had ever been before, and he thought that he probably would die if she ever removed her hands.

At first she stroked him gently while he kissed her deeply, but then she handled him more firmly and pressed both of her hands together around him in a manner that made him utter a small whimper, which seemed to please her.

"You will have to make a promise to me, before I continue," she whispered between the kisses without removing her hands.

"Anything you want," Quentin answered, dazzled. "Anything."

"The fox hunting in this forest has to stop," she said and carefully took her hands away from him. "Promise me that."

"Yes. Yes, I promise. No more fox hunting on this property ever again. Just do not stop, please," he said almost desperately, but a small part of him thought that it was a very strange request.

However, he abandoned the thought – all thoughts, really – as her hands started to touch and stroke him once again.

She gently pushed him on his back, and in the moon's dim light through the broken roof, she slowly straddled him. The moonlight fell on her naked breasts and hips and gleamed in her hair, which made it look like the ends of the red hair were painted with silver. Her hands rested on his chest and then slid down to help him enter her.

She was surprisingly wet and warm inside. She bent forward and kissed him once, twice and then she straightened up and rode him slowly. He touched her breast and reached up to kiss them as she increased her pace.

He caressed her breasts and licked one of her nipples when she suddenly dug her nails hard into his back and pushed faster against him. She let out a small scream, an animal-like sound, and he felt her tighten inside. This unexpected, sensual feeling, together with the increased pace and the pain from his bleeding back, caused him to come immediately.

He came deep inside her and pressed her body to his until it felt as if their two bodies had melted together and he was surrounded by an ocean of red hair with white tips.

*

The search party found Quentin during the first couple of hours after sunrise. He lay asleep under a fallen tree and was unharmed except for some bruises and several cuts on his back. Everyone agreed about that it was quite a miracle that he had survived the cold and rainy night at all.

The horse appeared near the stable the next day, but Quentin's red riding jacket was never found. His father was beside himself with happiness over his son's narrow escape from death. Indeed, he was so happy to see his son alive at all that he never even asked why he wanted them to end the foxhunting on the property.

The hunt had been a real disappointment anyway since nobody had been able to catch even a single fox. Quentin's father just assumed that the request was a result of the boy's trauma after surviving the cold November night during St Hubert's Day fox hunting.

* * *

~ Strange Masks ~

"Look! What is that, over there?" Isabella was pointing at an object under a dusty sheet in the corner of the attic, which turned out to be an old wooden chest. The two sisters and their cousin immediately tried to open it.

"It is stuck, it will not open!" said Mary, disappointed.

"Oh, step aside, little sister, and let me have a try," said Isabella. "After all, I was the one who found it."

"I think actually that I should have a try – after all, I am the oldest one here," interrupted Jane, their cousin, sweeping her brown curly hair out of her eyes.

After much debating and fussing, they managed to open the antique chest. The metal from the hinges creaked a little. They looked into the chest curiously, pushing each other to get a better look at its contents.

"What on Earth is that?" asked Mary.

"I- I do not know, really," said Jane, looking down at the face-shaped items in black and white.

"I know what it is!" Isabella cried out with triumph in her voice. "Look," she said and grabbed one of the objects and held it up in the weak light. "These are masks! Masks, which are meant to be used during a masquerade!"

The silence held for about three seconds, and then the two sisters and their cousin left the attic running down the stairs and screaming to each other.

*

Oh, no. The peace is over for today. Thomas Wilson sighed and lowered his newspaper as he heard the girls coming down the stairs and talking loudly to each other.

"Papa! Papa! You have to see what I found," yelled Isabella.

"Uncle Thomas, Uncle Thomas! Look at this!" screamed Jane, waving a mask above her head.

"Papa, can we please arrange a masquerade, please? Please say yes! You have to!" Mary added to the general ruckus as they stormed in to Thomas's study, a nice room with wooden panels, a large oriental rug and several bookcases filled with books.

Thomas closed the newspaper with another sigh. He was just reading about "The Great Exhibition" which had been held at the Crystal Palace in London, where attractions such as hydraulic presses and steam hammers had been on display.

"Girls! For heaven's sake, what are you talking about? And please, one at the time. You, Jane. My daughters are not making any sense – perhaps you could enlighten me?"

Both Isabella and Mary blushed, but Jane cleared her throat and said:

"Sir, we found an old chest in the attic. Inside we found strange masks of a curious design."

Isabella was waving one of the masks to show her father. It had an oversized beak instead of a normal nose and slanted slits for the eyes.

"And, well…" continued Jane. "We thought that maybe, if you do not think I am to bold to suggest it, we could hold a masquerade, here at the mansion, if you would agree of course." Both sisters were nodding enthusiastically behind Jane her to show their father what an excellent idea this was.

"A masquerade, you say…" Thomas mused with a blank expression. "I think I recognise those masks… I think that my grandfather brought with him from one of his trips to Venice. There was a story behind them, but I cannot remember it…" he trailed off, absently stroking his greying moustache.

"So, Father, is that a yes? Can we arrange a masquerade then?" asked Isabella in her sweetest voice.

"Please?" begged Mary and tilted her head to one side. "I mean, we had to cancel the spring reception because Mama took ill, and Isabella and I have never had the opportunity to wear the new evening dresses from London. Oh, and Jane will go back to Ipswich in just a couple of weeks," she added rapidly, realizing that her father would never ever grasp the full importance of dresses.

"Girls! Really!" said Thomas

The girls immediately fell silent and tried to look as well-behaved as possible, even though they were covered in dust and Isabella had spider webs in her hair.

Thomas looked at his two youngest daughters and his favourite niece and knew that he already had lost this battle. "I will talk to your mother about it," he continued and looked sternly at his daughters, who gave up a cry of disappointment echoed by Jane.

"A-ha! Only well-behaved daughters and nieces get to attend any possible future masquerades!" he said, interrupting their wailing.

"Yes, Father," said Isabella with a curtsy.

"Of course, Uncle Thomas," said Jane and made a curtsy as well.

"As you say, Father," added Mary and spread her dusty dress and made a curtsy too. "We do not want to disturb your studies any further, and we will leave you now. Thank you for taking your time with us. Come little sister and cousin, let us leave Father in peace", said Isabella and the young women left the room quietly.

Thomas sighed again.

*

"Do you really think Lord Barlow will come tonight?" asked Mary as she fidgeted with her fair, coiled hair in front of the dressing table.

"Is he not too old for you?" teased Isabella who was standing behind her, examining her own figure and the new emerald green evening dress in the mirror critically. "Maybe he is looking for an older, more mature woman."

"Oh! Like you ever are going to get married! You are already nineteen, practically an old hag!" screamed Mary and threw the hairbrush at Isabella, who ducked.

"Jane was nineteen when she married last summer, was she not?" Isabella retorted.

"Do not involve me in your argument, please," said Jane who was concentrating on putting on a golden necklace.

"What if I never get married?" said Mary in a worried voice.

"Yes, it must be a terrible fate. You will continue to live with our parents and never have children or your own family. But ask Jane, she knows all the tricks for a good match," said Isabella and helped Mary with her black and white mask. The mask was decorated with blue feathers that matched the sky-blue evening dress that Mary was wearing. She then helped Jane with her necklace.

"Thank you," said Jane. "And, well yes, I consider myself very fortunate that I got married last year." She smiled mischievously and added in a superior voice, "In fact, I would never ever want to spend so much energy on gossiping about future husbands like you do!"

"I beg your pardon!" Isabella exclaimed with a smile. "Well, then. Tell us about your marriage," she said slyly, adjusting her own mask with the long beak instead of a regular nose.

"You will have to find out for yourself one day," smiled Jane. "Oh! I forgot my mask in my room. I must go and collect it before the guests will start to arrive. I will meet you downstairs in a moment."

*

Jane lingered a while in her room before she went downstairs. She had been in this room every summer for as long as she could remember, but this was the first summer she had arrived as Mrs Campbell and not as Miss Lewis, and she could not help that deep down, she missed being Miss Lewis. The matrimonial bliss had yet to occur, but how could it ever do so when Mr Campbell never was around?

And what about children? Jane thought to herself, half mocking and half-sad. *How can there be any children if Mr Campbell is always travelling to London?*

Aunt Henrietta had carefully asked in the beginning of the summer if Jane had any delicate questions that could be discussed only between married ladies. Jane had said that she had no questions, and she had added that sometimes, certain things took longer time than others did. Sweet stout Aunt Henrietta, who had given birth to eight children, had given her a knowing smile, agreed and said that patience is a virtue.

Mr Campbell – my husband – is sweet and young, Jane thought and started to walk back and forth absentmindedly. *Not twice my age, which sometimes is the case for younger brides. He was also a very good catch, so everyone had agreed. I should be very grateful and nothing else. He also was quite handsome. Tall and slender, with clear green eyes and dark brown hair. What else could I possibly wish for?*

Jane sat down restlessly in a leathered winged chair. *Oh, Jane, be honest with yourself and stop acting like a girl. As a married woman, should you not admit – at least to yourself – that two attempts of…physical contact, during a whole year, might be too… seldom for a newly wedded couple?* That was the question she would have liked to ask Aunt Henrietta.

She thought about their wedding night. Oh, how she blushed at the memory. It had been a long day, with celebrations and all, until they finally had went to bed. Both of them had been nervous, she was sure about that, and she tried to make everything as easy as possible. She had lain completely still as Mr Campbell had taken of her nightgown and his own and kissed her gently while he spread her legs.

It had not been too bad, only hurt a little, and it had not lasted very long. She thought secretly, and perhaps wickedly, that maybe, just maybe, she might even enjoy it with some practice. But the months went by, and even although Jane went to bed early, she rarely had company. Mr Campbell usually sat up late in his study or went to London in business.

Before Christmas, when Mr Campbell had arrived back to Ipswich after a long business trip, they had repeated the procedure awkwardly. Mr Campbell sent wonderful gifts from London and seemed to enjoy her company, in a nervous way perhaps, but Jane could not help but wonder if he avoided her.

The sun was going down and the last rays cast long shadows over her old bed. She tied the long velvet ribbons behind her head and adjusted her chequered smiling mask with jester bells in front of her dressing table. For some reason it felt better wearing the smiling mask instead of her own smile. Downstairs it sounded as if the party already had begun.

*

Jane walked down the large stairs, looking for Mary and Jane, but realised the futility of it since everyone was wearing the black and white masks given to each guest upon their arrival. Even the serving men and the little orchestra in the corner were wearing them.

She managed to get a glass of punch that she sipped on while she searched for her cousins. She thought she recognised Isabella dancing, with her new green dress and long-nosed mask, and Jane decided to join the dance.

The dance was the classic dance that was held at practically all balls or social gatherings, but Jane thought that either the music played a little too fast or she had drunken the punch a little too swiftly, because in the corner of her eyes she kept seeing strange things going on. Every time she had tried to get a proper look, a new dancing partner, wearing a different mask, arrived in front of her and distracted her. She thought she caught a glance of two persons kissing, half hidden behind a curtain.

That could absolutely not be one of the servants kissing Mary, could it? Jane thought alarmed, after recognizing Mary's sky-blue dress from London together with her chequered mask, decorated with feathers. She had to end this dance immediately. She begged her next dancing partner pardon and stepped away, leaving her spot and a surprised woman behind her.

As she left the dance and finally had the opportunity to have a proper look around the room, she was shocked by the scene before her. The drawing room was large, and the dancing event and orchestra took up most of the space, but around it chairs were placed for guests resting or watching the dance while taking refreshments. This night however, the guests were acting odd, very odd indeed.

She could see a man and a woman, both wearing masks sitting – no, half lying! – on a loveseat while kissing each other in a most indiscrete way that was not suitable at parties. Even worse, a member of the orchestra lay on the floor and was straddled by a plump woman, and he was actually to Jane's shocked astonishment stroking the woman's breasts through the velvet fabric of her gown. No one seemed to mind or care.

"What is going on here?" she asked loudly. She tried not to look anywhere except at her feet as she approached the corner where she had sighted Mary.

"Going somewhere?" a man asked and grabbed her wrist as she passed by. She had not noticed the person as she walked by, but when she tried to turn, he took hold of her other arm so that it was impossible to turn around. "I have not seen you earlier tonight," he whispered in her ear.

"Please, let go off me instantly! I am terribly sorry to inform you but somehow everyone has gone quite mad. It could be something with the punch maybe…" She trailed off as the man leaned against her.

"But you do not want me to let go, now do you?" he said in her ear.

To her surprise, she realised that the unknown man was right. In fact, she wanted something else, something quite the opposite.

"Well, I… I must go to Mary! I think she is in trouble," she said nervously.

"But she is not. Look for yourself," the anonymous man said. She could feel his breath against her cheek.

He was right, at least in a way. Mary – if indeed it was Mary – was engaged with both the servant and one of the guests. One of the female guests.

She was sitting in front of Mary and kissing her tenderly, while the serving man was undoing the many buttons on the back of the sky-blue dress. Mary seemed to enjoy the experience, and one of her hands had slipped underneath the woman's elegant dress.

"Oh, my God, what are they doing? Someone should stop them..." Jane said, when she suddenly felt a hand moving slowly along her waist. Dazed, she looked down and saw that the hand was travelling along her waist until it reached her chest.

He is wearing a very expensive-looking pleated coat, she thought distractedly and struggled weakly to be free, but she managed only to press herself closer to the stranger holding her. She became conscious of the fact that she could feel his whole body against her back, which added to her confusion and growing pleasure.

This is wrong, she thought distantly, but abandoned the thought completely as her captor started to touch her breast. She wanted him to stop, but also at the exact same time she wanted him to continue!

She pressed herself firmly against him as he slid his fingers inside her mouth. She was pleased to hear him moan quietly as she started to lick his fingers. The moan grew to something else as she discovered that he liked also when she sucked on his fingers as they slid in and out of her mouth. His fingers left her mouth and she felt him undo her evening gown, which fell to the floor. He then let his hand wander under the many layers of her silk undergown while he gently rocked her back and forth against his hard body.

When she was ready to come, he brought her down on the floor and there, in front of everybody, and only half dressed, he entered her with slow, delicate determination. He continued to rock her rhythmically until she cried out and begged him to continue, to take her, to come inside her, without even knowing his name.

*

Epilogue One

The day after, in the backyard, they burned all the black and white masks together with the old wooden chest in which they had found them. No one ever spoke about all the dreadful and shameful things that had occurred, but quite a few remembered dimly what had happened, and it was agreed secretly and silently that it had been the best masquerade ever.

Epilogue Two

"Granny, Granny! Look what we have found in the attic."

* * *

~ View of a cemetery ~

October the 31ˢᵗ, 1853

"Dear diary," William wrote and looked out through the window. The rain had stopped momentarily but would probably come back with renewed strength, maybe as snow, later during the night. He took a sip of his tea and looked down on the nearly empty page in the diary and continued:

"Nearly a year has passed since I first met her. Strange, really, the way time flies. It feels only like yesterday," he wrote and lost himself in the memory. *Everything changed last year when Aunt Elizabeth decided to move to Bath, since the London air no longer agreed with her*, he thought.

He had been brought up by Aunt Elizabeth, to lessen the family shame; his mere existence had ruined every chance for his mother to be married. As the years passed by, William continued to live with Aunt Elizabeth, helping her with small errands while saving money for his own future marriage.

His connections were fairly good, much thanks to Aunt Elizabeth's influence; but as a natural child, he had to compensate economically if he wanted a beneficial marriage. He knew that he could not be regarded as handsome; he was too tall and slim, and his reddish hair, which indicated perhaps an Irish father, was not favourable either. Not that William himself really cared anymore; he was already seven and thirty, but Aunt Elizabeth cared enough for both of them and had not given up hope just yet.

It had nearly broken her heart when William had told her that he would not join her to Bath. Pleads and promises of social events, new introductions, theatres and dancing could not persuade him, and with a vow that he would come and visit every summer, he had seen the carriage leave London and then moved to his new apartment, located in a less fashionable district, within a week.

The chubby landlord had described the apartment as 'smart and quiet, well suitable for a young bachelor like yourself', and the rent was low. With two rooms, a small bedroom and a newly renovated bathroom, the apartment was more than William had ever hoped for. And quiet, yes indeed, with the rest of the property waiting for new tenants after the bathroom renovations, and with a view of the old Winchester's cemetery, nothing would probably disturb him or his writing.

During the same time that Aunt Elizabeth had started talking about moving to Bath permanently, William had, acting on an uncharacteristic whim, in all secret sent three of his best short novels to an editor. He had, of course, used a pseudonym. William was slightly embarrassed by his writing avocation, but he wrote nonetheless: Small poems or poetry, novels both short and long, William had been writing for as long as he could remember.

Days of anguish and remorse followed, until – to William's utmost surprise – the editor replied and wanted to meet him in person and discuss the production of ten short stories to be published in a rather well recognised magazine.

*

In his journal William wrote: "It is the small things which sometimes lead us to the great adventures." And indeed, had he not sent his novels to the editor, he probably would have moved with Aunt Elizabeth to Bath, and he would never had met his beloved.

He had rearranged the furniture in his apartment and converted the former dinner table to a writing and reading desk in front of the window in the sitting room. He did not plan to have any dinner parties or social gathering, so no one could object to the lack of a dinner table. Furthermore, he had placed the antique loveseat in front of the fire, where he now could have his meals and read.

With this clever arrangement, he could use most of the daylight and only had to use the firewood to heat up one of the rooms. The only thing that slightly bothered him was that the window in his study was facing the cemetery, but he making maximum use of daylight for work was not disrespectful, was it?

A couple of weeks went by and in the end of October, the first snow arrived and took London by surprise, which happened almost every year. William had been working late again, consumed by his writing, and he had completely forgotten his cold tea on the desk. He looked up from his writing to stretch his sore back, which made small complaining noises after hours of work.

A small flicker outside the window caught his attention. *Was it a light, a small lantern? Who could possibly be down at the graveyard lighting candles at this time?* he thought. *Or could it be… thieves? Grave robbers?* He shuddered, but then had to laugh at himself. All this writing had clearly stirred up his imagination! Still, he decided, it was his civil duty to go down there and investigate, so he put on his winter frock coat and leather gloves.

The street was deserted and covered in new snow. A few carriage trails could be seen in the snow, and William hesitated a moment in front of the iron gates at the entrance to the cemetery, suddenly torn between the battle of Comfort and Curiosity. Comfort allied itself with Common Sense, which said that entering a graveyard after dark could be a folly, but both nonetheless lost against Curiosity.

Just a short visit, and then back to the study, William promised himself as he walked along the walking path, buried in snow.

The cemetery rested in the shadows of large unpruned trees. William walked slowly along the snow-covered path, which was framed by old brittle graves in various stages of degradation. He tried to read the old inscriptions on the graves, some dating back at least two hundreds years, and some with unreadable engravings were probably older still.

William was just about to turn around and leave, thinking that his civilian righteousness had been paid, when he caught sight of something in the corner of his eye. In the monochrome-coloured graveyard, a little red candle had been placed on top of a small tombstone just at the edge of the light from the streetlamp.

The candle was not burning anymore, William noticed as he approached, but the small grave was uncovered from snow and cleared from moss and old leaves. The rest of the cemetery seemed neglected; apparently no gardener had visited the graveyard for ages, however someone was tending this tomb.

Lucy Ann Whitaker
3rd of April 1762 ~ 11th of December 1781
Beloved daughter and fiancée
"Our Angel, Rest in Peace."

So poor young Miss Whitaker still has someone who cares for her, William thought. She had been engaged, but her fiancé must be at least ninety by now and her parents must surely be dead. Maybe a devoted younger sister or another relative came here to tend her grave.

But why light candles at the tomb at this time? It did not make any sense.

Well, at least no one has desecrated the graves, quite the opposite, William thought as snow started to fall through the thin autumn foliage above him. He hesitated, then took off his glove and bent down to touch the candle. *Hm, the wax is still soft and warm. Someone has been here in the past few minutes, probably less.* William looked around with the strange feeling of being watched. *Is Miss Whitaker's relative still here?*

William suddenly felt vulnerable and cold. His feet sent silent complaints concerning their discomfort. He walked fast towards the ornamented iron gates and the warm light from the burning gas light along the street. But with one hand on the gate, he turned around again, uncertain.

"Hello?" he called out, feeling silly but also, inexplicably, a little afraid.

"Is there someone there?" he continued and took a step away from the gate. He thought he saw something – someone – standing in the shadows behind one of the trees. Yes, there was someone there, a woman, he was sure, and he took another step forward.

"Eh, my name is William. I… ah, live nearby…" he said, not knowing what to say. Surely the lady must be numb with cold; it certainly could not be healthy to be outdoors in this wretched weather.

He was closer now, just a couple of yards away. It was indeed a young woman, pale with long brown entangled hair, a torn, old-fashioned dress and naked feet. She was standing half-hidden behind a tree. She was maybe twenty years old, small and feminine, with a perfectly oval shaped face and large brown eyes.

"Leave me, William," he heard her say in a low voice, but of course he could not do that. This was clearly a lady in distress. He took another step forward and gently offered his arm to the young woman hiding in the shadows.

"My lady, I mean you no…"

William never had the possibility to finish his sentence; it all happened too quickly. One second he was reaching out towards the young lady, and in the next moment, she charged at him. He fell backwards, sprawled in the snow, as she bent over him. "Forgive me," he thought he heard her say, and he felt her ice-cold hands embrace him and a small sharp pain against his neck. Reality went black.

Blood coloured the white snow red.

*

"Oh my God! My God, what have I done? Please St Mary, let him live, for all that is holy…"

"…I did not mean it, I am so, so sorry."

"William? William? Can you hear me?"

He was so cold. And so tired. He drifted back into oblivion.

*

"Tea, sir?" she asked and offered him a cup of steaming hot tea.

"Thank you," said William weakly and sipped from the hot beverage.

He felt as if he was waking up from a dream, disoriented and confused. He was lying on the loveseat under several blankets and a young, pretty lady was sitting in his armchair by the table.

"Eh, my apologies, but who are you? And what happened… at the cemetery?" His memories started to come back to him, but they did not make any sense.

"No offence taken, sir. My name is Miss Lucy Whitaker and I am afraid I… attacked you. I did bring you here though, afterwards I mean, and I think you will…" She hesitated and added, "Ah… get well," but William had a growing feeling that she had meant to say something completely different.

Lucy sat curled up in the armchair staring into the fire as she continued. "This is my story. I was born in 1762 and I died nineteen years later in 1781. I do not know how exactly… I was waiting for my betrothed Jacques, outside the theatre. He was a little late, and suddenly someone grabbed me from behind, and that is more or less the only thing I remember. Since then, I have haunted the cemetery, afraid to leave. A half-ghost, not accepted to enter heaven, but not condemned to hell either."

She paused and stole a quick glance in his direction before resuming her story: "Winchester's cemetery was old already in the end of the eighteenth century. I have walked it for decades feeding on small animals and stray pets. It has had few visitors over the years and yesterday was the first time I... I... attacked someone. I am so utterly sorry," she said, her voice full of sorrow.

"My lady, are you saying you are a... a vampire? A beast...or a demoness?" William could not help but ask. This beautiful young woman in a torn burial dress was the tainted one? An embodiment of Lilith herself? "Will I become like you now?" William asked carefully.

"No, I... do not think so. You see, I died and then I woke up again, while you merely ...got ill. But you survived, thank God," she said and he saw two trails of tears leave her eyes.

"My lady. Eh, Miss Whitaker. Please, do not cry," he said awkwardly and rose a little unsteadily from the loveseat.

"Do not come near me!" she exclaimed and sunk away from him in the large leather armchair.

"It is all right, my lady," he said and patted her shoulder. The young woman was clearly deranged, but he would do anything to make this little beautiful creature stop crying and soothe her grief.

"But you do not understand," she sobbed unhappily. "I want you near me. I want your touch and... I... I crave you."

She looked up into his eyes. Her pupils were completely dilated and dark.

She was so warm, he realised, as he touched her shoulder. So warm and young. And so… female. She even smelled good. Under the earthy leaf smell she smelled like… like a kitten, sleeping in the sun. Her tangled hair was soft to the touch. He stroked her curls and placed a tangled lock behind her ear.

"There, there," he said soothingly.

"William, if you do not leave me right this second, I am not responsible for my actions, neither as a damned creature nor as a former member of the weaker sex!" she said, her voice strangled.

"Hush, my lady, you are not really well…" William said and patted her shoulder again. The poor young woman was clearly disturbed and probably hurt as well.

"…Not responsible for my actions…" she whispered slowly and stood up, tip-toe, and kissed him.

He was too surprised to draw back. When he tried, she had already placed her unexpectedly strong arms around his neck and he lacked the strength to pry them away. In fact, he felt strangely helpless, as if it were someone else who acted instead of him as he kissed her in return. His hands involuntarily reached her waist and pulled her closer.

She, on the other hand, shredded his clothes as if they were made of paper and pulled him down towards the floor with him on top of her. She kissed him deeply while he fumbled with her dress and struggled with the endless buttons. He wanted her desperately.

Having been a lifelong bachelor with little sexual experience, except for a few embarrassing acts in his youth, he was almost delirious with lust. Gone was etiquette and shyness; left were only the burning need and desire to be with her, to enter her and take her.

And finally, the last pieces of clothing were removed and she lay, naked and perfect with her back arched, in front of the fireplace on the wooden floor. He wanted to savour the moment but it was impossible to resist; he entered her with a small cry that was matched by her soft scream.

He kissed her again and stroked her perfect apple-shaped breasts, complete with small, mischievous pink nipples, as he continued to push against her. She entangled her legs around his waist and kissed him back, her fingers intertwined in his hair.

The feeling of her round and full breasts and hard small nipples, and the wet and warm sensation as he moved against her, together with the sight of her beauty as she lay underneath him in the light from the fire, made him increase his pace.

He knew he would come soon, without any possibility to stop himself or to withdraw, when suddenly she came with a small growl. He came a second after her, as he knew he would, deep inside her, uncontrollably and with a pleasure that bordered on insanity.

As he collapsed on top of her, he felt the familiar sharp pain against his neck, and as he once again drifted off towards unconsciousness, he thought he heard her say his name.

*

He woke up again, numb with cold and under all the blankets on the loveseat but without his clothes. Lucy was there, warm beside him with almost flustered cheeks. William sighed blissfully and looked down on her as she lay with her head on his chest.

"Who are you, really, I mean?" he asked.

"I told you. My name is Miss Lucy Whitaker, born in 1762," she said quietly.

"Mmm…And what are you exactly?"

"Does it matter?" she asked, large brown eyes looking into his.

"No…" he answered truthfully, kissing her forehead. "It does not."

The world was truly a mystery, and he realised that he was strangely and utterly in love.

*

A year later, and still so very much in love, William wrote in his journal.

The sun was going down, the shadows extended. She preferred to stay at the cemetery during daytime; claiming it made her feel safe.

She will be here in a short while, William thought.

He wrote one last sentence in the diary before he closed it:

"I do not know how long time we will have together, or what will happen in the future, but I am happy here and now, and perhaps that is all that matters…"

William put the journal down and went to stand by the window with the view of the cemetery. In a couple of minutes, after dusk, he would be able to see her walking between the graves and then open the ornamented iron gates to the cemetery. The wait seemed to last an eternity.

* * *

~ Master and Servant ~

Velvet curtains hung from the antique four-poster mahogany bed. In his dream, hands travelled along his chest, teasing and caressing his shivering flesh. He lay on his back, naked, vulnerable and completely erect as the hands continued their voyage down towards his stomach, and he moaned with expectation.

"Do you want me to continue?" a husky voice mumbled in his ear as the fingers journeyed along the inside of his thighs. But something was wrong, he realised in the fog of pleasure as the delicate fingers started to stroke the full hard length of the most sensitive region of his body.

The voice was… male.

*

His eyes flew open.

James lay, entangled by a wrinkled mess of blankets and sheets, in his own bed. He was alone, he realised with a mixed sense of relief and, before he could stop himself, disappointment. And, while being sweaty and still hard from the dream, he was still dressed in a proper nightshirt. He fell back into the pillows and sighed.

Dawn was creeping through the window, painting the room in the weak sepia of day. His thoughts lingered at the memory of the dream, remembering perhaps more than he would like to admit. For a short second he thought about giving in, finding he own release, but he denied himself. He did not thing it would be wise to encourage these wicked, involuntary dreams.

A cold shower, a walk, and perhaps an early riding tour will be the best cure, he thought guiltily as he splashed water on his face and looked himself in the mirror, getting ready to shave. He was nine-and twenty now, with small lines on his forehead, but no laugh lines. *I look older, or perhaps it is just the restless sleep that makes me look more tired and paler than usual,* he speculated as he reached for the shaving kit.

He quickly left the large mansion for his morning walk. The mist was still dancing on the fields and the birds had just started their morning serenade to celebrate another beautiful spring day on the countryside. He walked briskly, stretching his long legs and letting his mind stray. As always, his thoughts took the well-travelled road of depression, this time choosing economy as the main headline of his thoughts.

His heritage, the huge neglected Kent mansion, was bleeding money, but leaving it – selling it – was not an option. He survived on small-scale horse and dog breeding business and on occasionally selling some of the estate's antique furniture or paintings.

He only had one servant now, since George, a true butler who had worked for him and his father (bless him), had retired. James was not entirely sure if he really appreciated his replacement. The new servant, Victor was his name, had arrived a month ago and was a relative to George.

He lacks all the familiar elegance that George had. Still, he is young and strong and more suitable for the hard work of taking care of the horses, James thought as he approached the stable and the end of his walk.

As he got closer, he heard someone whistling. James did not recognise the melody, but it sounded like a merry folksong of some kind. He hesitated and then continued forward, slower and more quietly, not wanting to disturb the working servant who obviously believed himself to be alone.

The servant, grooming a horse, was standing with his back towards James. He had taken his shirt off and placed it on the nearby fence. James froze, unable to look away from the servant's undressed back. He felt an odd surge through his body. The servant had tanned broad shoulders with a thin film of sweat that covered his working muscles as he groomed the black horse at a steady pace. He was still whistling, unaware of James, but the horse, a full-blooded stallion with a nervous temper, noticed James and tossed its head, which made the servant to turn around.

"Oh. I beg your pardon, did I interrupt you?" said James with a nervous laugh.

"No, sir, not at all. Beautiful morning, is it not?" Victor replied friendlily. He was in his early twenties, with blond, slightly untidy hair and dark green sparkling eyes.

His lady friends probably describe him as very handsome, James pondered.

"I took Ebony for a short exercise trip down the lake, but I can make him ready, should you prefer to ride out," the servant added, continuing with the grooming. His chest and abdomen looked as if they were sculptured from dark granite and he wore some kind of leather necklace.

"Yes! I-I think I would like that," James said rapidly. "I will wait by the courtyard, then," he added abruptly and walked away briskly.

He waited impatiently until Victor brought Ebony, now bridled and saddled. Victor had put on his shirt again, James noticed, confused by his own disappointment.

Their hands did not touch as Victor gave the reins to James, but the difference between their hands, so close together, was striking. James's long, slender and pale fingers beside Victor's larger hand, covered with calluses and small blond hairs on the knuckles.

"When do you want the carriage to be ready, sir?" asked Victor.

"Pardon?"

"The carriage? You do plan to attend Lord and Lady Hastings's event tonight, do you not?" said Victor.

"Oh. Yes. But of course. Around eight would be appropriate, I guess," James said, his tone revealing his complete lack of interest in the Hastings's spring ball.

"I will have it ready for you. Should I come to your room after dinner and help you prepare then?" Victor asked.

"Yes… After dinnertime will be suitable. Please brush the dark blue coat and iron a suitable shirt," James said with a perhaps somewhat strangled voice.

"Have a nice ride, sir," said Victor as James sat up and took the reins.

"Thank you," James answered shortly and urged the horse into a brisk trot.

What is wrong with me? James thought as he rode away. First the odd dream and now this. His imagination was playing tricks with his mind and making his behaviour erratic. He did not understand himself.

Victor stood by the courtyard and saw James ride away. He allowed himself a small sigh before he went back to work and daydreaming.

*

Later James paced his room back and forth nervously. Dusk had come, and he had lit candles and an oil lamp on the table close to the bed. The high mansion windows were ajar and the wind played slowly with the long curtains. He was wearing dark grey breeches and a linen shirt. His formal evening garments were in the care of the servant.

Finally Victor arrived, carrying the evening's clothes and shoes.

"Ah, there you are," James said when Victor carefully closed the door behind him.

"Sir," mumbled Victor as he laid out the clothes on the sitting table and put the polished shoes on the floor.

"Eh, sir," victor asked as James made no sign of moving and seemed temporarily lost in thoughts. "Do you mind taking that shirt off, sir, so you can put on the ironed one?"

"Yes, of course!" James said, a little forced. He removed his shirt and stood bare-chested in the candlelight.

He is so pale and slim. Almost like a marble statue, Victor thought, fussing with the shirt by the table. He removed the white starched linen shirt from the rest of the clothes and carefully let it slip on James, making sure that it did not get wrinkled in the process.

They stood opposite of each other as Victor slowly buttoned all the buttons all the way up. Victor dressed James in the cream-coloured breeches next and donned the white stockings. He then went back to the table to get the muslin cravat. His fingers brushed James throat as he tied it gently.

"Shoes next, sir," Victor said, wondering a little over his master's silence. *Was he unsatisfied with the ironing? Had he done something wrong?*

Victor collected the black shoes with silver buckles and went down on his knees in front of James. He smoothly slipped on one shoe, his hands resting a second on James ankle before donning the other shoe, and then stood up. He was slightly shorter than James, he realised as he stole a glance of his master. He went back to the table, gathered a waistcoat this time, and unhurriedly put it on, his fingers just touching James's shoulders and waist as he corrected the fit.

"Just the coat left," Victor said to himself, slowly sliding it on and, for extra precaution, made sure that no dust had settled on the dark blue fabric. He gently turned James around towards the large mirror by the window.

"You look extraordinary," he said as he stood beside James. Then Victor silently cursing himself; servants were not meant to talk this much.

James looked at himself in the mirror. He looked pale and strained, like a porcelain doll beside a living person. The contrast between them was stunning. Victor in his natural beauty and healthy colour; himself a pale shadow, slender and thin, dressed in the latest fashion.

Letting someone dress him and being so close to another person was uncommon for James. The old butler had never dressed him for any occasion, just silently delivered the perfectly ironed clothes. But this, this was something else. It felt as if his skin was tingling where Victor accidentally had touched him.

"Is there anything else I can do for you, sir?" Victor asked. He noticed that James eyes had the strangest expression and that his master's breathing was just a little bit short. He innocently continued to search for imaginary dust particles, tempting fate and perhaps himself.

"Anything else, sir?" he said and just slightly leaned closer, while his mind was rebelling against his behaviour. What was he doing? Was he insane? He would lose his employment! Ah, but he had not done anything wrong. Not yet.

"Anything, sir... What do you want me to do?"

"Seduce me," James whispered back, breathlessly.

"As you wish, Master," Victor said softly, as he gave free rein to his yearning and kissed him lightly.

The kiss started gently, lips touching wet lips in short breaths, but as hands explored flesh, the kiss grew deeper and tongues met. They kissed again and half wrestled towards the old four-poster bed, ripping the bed curtains aside. A formerly perfectly ironed linen shirt landed on the floor, soon followed by a servant's simple brown shirt.

For James, this was a vivid dream; he refused to acknowledge reality and without any remorse lost himself in his most secret of guilty pleasures. His body taught him everything he needed to know and it guided him easily. He wanted to kiss and be kissed.

It was so easy to give in, especially since he noticed that Victor was responding with a physical need as strong as his own was. The sound of Victor moaning as they kissed made James bold, and he could not resist the temptation to move closer as they lay on the bed.

He felt their bodies connect and his own hardness touch Victor's, with just a couple of thin layers of clothes between them. Victor pushed his hips closer and tanned hands gently glided down towards his belt.

"Lie still and close your eyes…" Victor mumbled as his hands removed the tailored breeches and the rest of his clothes.

James closed his eyes, blocking out the candlelight. All he heard was his own uneven breathing. His heart raced and he sighed with eager anticipation as more experienced fingers moved along the inside of his legs and ran over his hardness. He felt Victor move and suddenly, as fingers gripped him, he felt an unexpected wetness covering him.

In his surprise he looked down, meeting mischievous eyes, but the enormous sensation of this new kind of kiss made him close his eyes again. He resisted pushing his hips forward and tried to lie still.

Victor's inquisitive fingers slipped back and forward; they held him in a firm grip, teasing him in conspiracy with wet lips. It was completely and utterly irresistible, and as James tentatively moved his hips forward, he was rewarded with a new wave of satisfaction.

Victor's fingers continued their adventure and stroked his full length up and down harder and more rapidly. James kept up with this new pace, knowing that this kind of pleasure was both forbidden and wrong.

Just the thought that "it was forbidden" made him realise that he had already lost: His desire had the upper hand and he would come during this unchristian and prohibited act, and he could not care less. But he wanted the most of it.

It took two tries before James managed to say the words. "Wait," he said with a hoarse voice.

Victor looked up curiously, his lips and fingers still surrounding James.

James moved so that he stood up on his knees in the bed, naked and with glistering erection.

"Like this?" he suggested, blushing with both timidity and lust.

Victor smiled and kneeled before him, his hands finding their place again and his tongue licked the very top of him, slowly, oh, so slowly.

"Tell me…" Victor said roguishly. When James gasped, he continued to lick at a deliberately slow pace. "…when you want me to make you come," he added teasingly.

James did not hesitate. He burrowed his hands in the blond hair and slightly forced Victor to increase the speed.

"Now. Please! God, now!" he cried out as he pushed himself forward. His quickened pace was met, and the wet pressure around him increased as fingers surround him.

James tried to pull back but Victor would not let him, so James came inevitably and deeply with a suppressed cry of satisfaction. He tumbled back among the pillows, panting and staring with unseeing eyes.

"Did you like it?" Victor asked, a little smug.

"Yes, very much…thank you," James gasped, cuddling closer so that his head rested on Victor's chest. "What is this?" he added, feeling suddenly shy, playing with an odd-looking stone placed in a leather cord around Victor's neck.

"Mmm… It is a lucky charm," Victor said, moving his firm body closer to James. "I bought it from some gypsies at a market before I moved here."

"Is it working?" James asked curiously.

"Well, yes. I think so," Victor answered, a little breathless. "Maybe it grants wishes as well," he added, gently guiding James hands…

* * *

~ Booklover ~

Elizabeth had travelled the world. At the tender age of eighteen she had already been to France many times, she had roamed Italy, and she had even visited Egypt and the exotic West Indies. She had travelled by horse, by train and by modern aircraft machines.

She had seen strange places and met wonderful people, some of which even had led to romantic liaisons. Indeed, she had danced with Mr Darcy, flirted with Mr Rochester and even had had a love affair with Mr George Knightley himself one summer. All this without even leaving the library at the family estate, the Abbey in Somerset.

She is there right now, in fact, but instead of reading or daydreaming, she is walking angrily back and forth on the thick oriental carpets.

*

"I cannot believe this!" I said aloud just to hear my own voice. To make sure I was not dreaming I even pinched myself. It hurt, so maybe this nightmare was real after all. Earlier I had walked past my parents' sitting room on the way to top floor where the library is located. The door happened to be a little open, probably left unclosed by a neglectful servant, and I was about to close it when I heard my name mentioned.

First I thought it was my father who had noticed me and wanted me to enter, but then I heard the rest of the conversation, and since it concerned me, I decided to not reveal my presence and instead carefully listened to the hateful dialogue that followed. It is not really eavesdropping if the conversation concerns yourself and your future happiness!

"Eliza is a little bit too young, according to me," I heard my father mutter.

"Oh, nonsense, my dear! She is eighteen, a perfect age for marriage in my opinion," my mother's high soprano voice replied.

Marriage? I thought alarmed and moved closer to the door.

"Oh, John," I heard my mother continue. "I know she is our youngest daughter and our favourite! Indeed I never thought we were going to have more children at my age, and she is such a blessed child! But a secured marriage between Eliza and Jonathan would solve the whole inheritance issue, and we would be sure that Eliza's future is properly secured and that the Somerset Abbey would still stay within the family. You know this, my dear."

Jonathan? Which Jonathan? They could not possibly mean... But my fears were confirmed when my father said ominously:

"You are right, I know. It is just… Jonathan is so much older and a little… stiff. I wished that Eliza would make a better match with someone more energetic, with a little bit spirit and adventures to lure her away from all her quiet reading, if you see what I mean?"

"My dear, we will never find someone that is good enough for our Eliza. But Jonathan Rupert is a good match. Trust me in this."

I fled at that moment, having heard the finality in my mother's voice. I was going to be married off to my revolting, boring and insufferable cousin, who was more than twice my age, to make sure the Abbey stayed in the family!

"Please, dear God, have mercy on me. Anyone, but not Jonathan," I prayed as I climbed the stairs. He had greasy black hair and always pinched my cheek, even after that I got too old for it. No wonder he was not married; he was too tall and too thin; he looked like a goat; and he had no sense of humour, intelligence (well, all right then, he was rather clever), but he did not have even one drop of romantic blood in his veins!

Not that I was a beauty; with my short and quite plump appearance and hopeless straight fair hair, I may at the most be considered pretty, but still!

The best part with books is that they do not judge you by the cover, I thought hopelessly as I finally entered the library. I was still furious and I walked angrily back and forth in my library mulling over my parents' conversation. It was, of course, not really my library, but for most of the time it was used solely by me. It was a perfectly wonderful room, filled with dark wooden bookshelves which were built-in along the panelled walls. It even had a movable iron staircase that I used to play with when I was younger.

My mother used to come here to read to me, and it was in this room I had learnt my first letters at the age of four. However, this evening, despite the oriental carpets, the burning candelabras, and the old family portraits, it felt like a prison.

I tried to imagine myself as a heroine, faced with a horribly fate which I was going to resist and in the end succeed to overcome, however I failed miserably. I did not want to marry cousin Jonathan! Indeed, I did not want to marry anyone. I just wanted to continue being Eliza. Little, quiet, slightly queer Eliza who always quoted her books. Instead, I was going to be turn into "Mrs Rupert", who by all accounts would only worry about dinner parties and lazy servants for the rest of her wretched life.

Finally I gave up. I was still angry (with the disagreeable cousin Jonathan, my parents, the Abbey and the world itself) but I decided to leave the library. No answers could be found here.

After I blew out all the candles, I slammed the door in frustration to my former sanctuary. I instantly regretted my childish behaviour, and my misery increased as I heard a muffled "thump" from inside.

Oh no! Have I broken something? What if one of the old paintings has fallen down? I took a candle from the hall and stepped back inside the library, which was waiting in darkness; it was after all rather late.

All the windows were closed properly and no damaged portrait could be seen. *So where did the sound come from?* I wondered as I tiptoed around in the library. At last I found the source of the commotion: A large leather-bound book had fallen down from one the upper shelves. It lay on the floor, just beside the antique rotating wooden Earth globe. The book was closed - and thank the Lord! - unharmed. In the candlelight I noticed that it had a beautiful front cover, with rich decorations that reminded me of the book "One Thousand and One Nights".

I could not find the book's proper place in the dim light, so I decided to bring it to my room and replace it in the morning. All the books had once been carefully organised by my mother; while most of the books belonged to my father, it was mainly the women in our family who read. The fact that I had no restrictions and was allowed to read whatever I fancied may sound strange to you, but at the time it made perfect sense to me.

Carrying the leather-bound book and without any more accidents, I went back to my room and straight to bed. All the anger had drained me of energy and I feel asleep almost instantly after a short session of crying with the book forgotten at my bedside table.

*

The book had waited for decades to find a new Reader, but it had not waited in vain.

Presently, the book listened to the young sleeping woman and thought, *Ah, a blossom girl, ready to unfold. A virgin, who had lost some of her shyness but still claimed her innocence.*

Marvellous, absolutely marvellous! I have chosen wisely.

*

My dreams were strange that night, and I woke before dawn. With the growing light I went through my limited options regarding my parents' horrible secret marriage plans. For the better part of an hour I lay there unable to reach any conclusions, and then I decided to take a long early morning walk before breakfast.

As I got ready, I noticed the odd book from the night before. I sat down on the bed and opened its ornamented covers. "Secrets of the Far East" was its intriguing title. It smelled old and faintly of exotic spices.

I started to read and became completely absorbed. The book was like nothing else I had ever read and contained several short novels with wonderful illustrations.

The stories, however, were slightly... quirky. At first, I thought it was a storybook for older children, however after a while it occurred to me that this kind of short stories may indeed be unsuitable for unwedded readers. I hid the book, but I read on each night and studied the illustrations with increasingly blushing cheeks.

The days that followed where filled with eavesdropping and spying. I gleaned information regarding the dreadful prospect wedding, but also overheard an innuendo conversation between my mother and my older sister regarding matrimonial deeds and duties.

More plain was the servants' gossip, to which I listened while standing under the kitchen window. Apparently one of the servant girls was having regular meetings with a gardener in the old barn during her nights off. What they were actually doing during these possibly immoral meetings was drowned in suppressed giggles, so I decided boldly to find out more.

I arrived well before dusk and hid myself behind a massive oak, close to the old barn. Soon after, the young and pretty servant girl came walking together with the sunset. Through the barn's little window, I could see her light a hooded lantern which she hung on a rusty peg on one of the wooden posts. She then spread out over the hay a checked blanket which she had brought, took out her braids and shook out her thick brown hair.

She was wearing a servant's simple dress, but in that moment she was strikingly beautiful and I felt a little bit embarrassed as she adjusted her dress so that more of her pale bosom was exposed. She sat down by the little window at the door with her back turned against me and we both held watch over the path. It started to rain quietly, a late summer drizzle that made me wrap my cloak more tightly around me.

It was almost full dark when I could see the silhouette of the gardener walking upon the path. He was older than the servant girl, broad of shoulders and with dark hair and tanned skin. As he entered the barn, I slowly and carefully drew closer to the window. My precaution was entirely wasted since the couple would never have noticed me, twenty galloping horses or a smaller earthquake.

As soon as the gardener had closed and blocked the large wooden door, the servant girl pulled him against her and they joined in the most lavish kiss I had ever witnessed or envisioned. Kisses, in my inexperienced world, were supposed to be light and tender. This, however, was the full-blown version, hot and breathless and with eager, exploring tongues.

As they kissed, he started to pull down her dress while mumbling how much he had missed her until her bare breasts where exposed. She had quite large and fair breasts which he kissed eagerly, licking the nipples until they became hard and she was moaning with pleasure.

"Are you ready?" he asked, stroking and kissing her nipples.

"Yes, please!" she said, panting, and started to pull at his trousers.

"No, no, none of that…" he said teasingly, but reluctantly, as he moved her hands away. "Not yet," he added and smiled roguishly at her disappointed sigh.

I stayed petrified in front of the window as the scene continued before me. I felt feverish and out of breath, wishing with all my heart that someone would make love to me like that, but I was also keenly aware of that I was watching something very private and that it was both wicked and wrong of me to stay and look. However, I did not – could not! – leave.

The servant girl was now entirely naked and lay back with her autumn brown hair spread out on the blanket. The gardener had lost his linen shirt, but he was still wearing his trousers. He was quite muscular and they lay side by side, with her back pressed against his front body.

One of his hands was occupied with caressing her breasts while his other hand had nestled down between her legs. Her eyes were closed and she rocked her body against his at the same rhythm as he moved his fingers. He kissed and licked her earlobe and whispered something that I almost could not hear:

"Now, now, darling. Now you are ready…"

"Mmm, please. I do anything for you," she mumbled and added, "Take me, or I will come anyway."

"Lay still, then," he said softly and stood up in front of her.

As she was letting her own hands replace his and touched herself slowly, he undressed completely.

My hands flew up and I quieted a little scream. I had never seen a man naked before, and to see him so, so *ready* sent a quiver through my entire body that ended deep inside of me.

I yearned with denied pleasure as he ordered her with a smile, "Move lass, and let me lay down, and then you can do what you please with me."

They changed positions, and to my shock the girl started to kiss and lick the most private part of his body until he grunted and pushed her away, which made her giggle mischievously.

"Come here," he said, laughing, and then wrestled her around so that she was straddling him. He reached up and kissed her breasts, and she moaned with pleasure and gently pushed him inside.

He arched his back and gripped her bottom eagerly, pulling her towards him and saying:

"Yes! Finally! Oh, I have missed you so much!"

Soon they were both sweaty and they took turns teasing each other. She sucked on his fingers passionately as she rode him thoroughly. In return, he kissed and pinched her nipples while he cradled her sweaty breasts.

In the end, their rhythm increased as she was straddling him, shoving her hips against his, and then suddenly she froze and screamed out, and seconds afterwards he said with a strained voice:

"Now! Now!"

He pulled out, and she stroked his hardness up and down repeatedly until he came with a small cry.

"What are you doing with me, woman?" he panted happily afterwards. "Now that, that was close," he added with a blissful smile and kissed her forehead. "We do not want any babies until we are properly married, do we?"

"I am sorry", she said with a small impish smile.

And I left them there, in their happiness. They were unaware of my present, their unknowingly granted love lesson, as well as the idea that they had given me.

*

Two month later, while still pretending to consider cousin Jonathan's marriage offer, I seduced my first and only victim: A wonderful boy at my own age with caramel-coloured eyes, curly brown hair and the cutest smile. We did not speak much, since we were from such different social classes, and he only stayed during his work for the summer.

No one had informed him about proper precautions regarding love making for unwedded couples, and a few months after our separation, I delivered the disastrous news to my shocked parents, who believe my innocent story about a very naive but unfortunate accident, and mostly blamed themselves for their Victorian silence regarding certain intimate matters.

Nevertheless, little Theodore was born in the beginning of the following year, when I was "taking art lessons" in France. At the same time, my barren older sister and her husband had the opportunity to adopt a young orphan boy from a distant relative.

Theodore grew up to become quite spoiled but happy, and he spent all his summers at his grandparent's Abbey in Somerset where I lived the rest of my days surrounded by my best friends in the library at the top floor.

* * *

~ The portrait of Mrs Elliott ~

"You have met my wife, Mrs Elliott, before, I presume?" the tall and stout tradesman inquired, waving in the general direction of his wife who stood half-hidden behind him.

"No, I do not believe I have had the pleasure, sir," I answered.

"There, there, love. Do not be shy now. This gentleman is going to paint your picture; you cannot hide from him," Mr Elliott said, laughing loudly and almost pushing her forward so that I stood face to face with her.

She was very petite, reaching only just below my shoulders, and she had large almond eyes, ivory skin and a slightly determined arched nose that suggested a continental heritage. And indeed, as she whispered her "How do you do, sir?" and bent her head, I heard a hint of an unmistakably French accent.

I bowed, and even though she probably was twice my age and clearly nervous, I felt a little shy myself.

"Well, darling dear," said her husband, "I will leave you with the artist and send the carriage in an hour. I'm going to the Traders' meeting and I will probably be late tonight. Bye now, and good luck with the painting, Basil!" And before any of us had the chance to react, Mr Elliott had dashed off.

We stood awkwardly for a minute or so in silence before we both said in chorus:

"Would you like to have some tea, Madame?"

"I wonder if it is going to rain later today?"

I blushed, let out a nervous laughter, and offered her to sit down at the round table in the drawing room while I arranged for tea.

While I was waiting for the water to boil, I mentally went over what I knew about Mr and Mrs Elliott. I had met Mr Albert Elliott at a social gathering, where I tried to mingle in the vain attempt to make the upper class society take notice of me, which in turn may result in painting orders.

So far, during this season in Bath, I had only had a few orders, so I was delighted when a slightly over-intoxicated Mr Elliott approached me and asked without any further introductions if I was a talented painter, and if so, whether I was willing to paint a portrait of his wife.

Apparently he had already had his own picture painted by a famous (and quite possibly a rather more expensive) painter. Nevertheless, a week later, a note was sent to me to decide the first date for a series of sittings.

So, what else did I know? Well, according to the not-so-flattering rumours, Mr Elliott was a man who enjoyed life to the fullest, including gambling, drinking, and women. A hard businessman, who had made a fortune in trading with the colonies, and had made a clever match with an aristocrat from Marseille. Less was known about this mysterious Mrs Joan Elliott who currently was sitting in my drawing room, waiting for tea and biscuits.

She must have been very young when she entered marriage, I mused while adding tea leaves into the kettle, since they had three sons together, all in their twenties, and, according to common knowledge, apparently Mr Elliott had had at least the same number of illegal offspring. Mrs Elliott, however, was not known to the society, and apparently avoided any social gatherings.

I placed the teapot, two porcelain cups and almond biscuits on a blue tray, and then went back to the drawing room where I found her sitting in almost the exact position as I left her.

She was sitting on the edge of the gold and yellow sofa, in a completely erect position, with her lace-gloved hands neatly folded in her lap. She looked up at me very quickly and then went back to inspecting the pattern of the aged carpet that covered most of the floor.

"I have made tea," I said, stating the obvious, and added, "Oh, and I have some almond biscuits, if you like." I poured the tea and placed the plate with biscuits within her reach. She gave me another shy glance and then carefully took the smallest biscuit and nibbled at its corner.

"Thank you, sir," she said, sipping the tea.

*

It took almost three whole sessions before I made her relax enough to start making basic charcoal sketches, and perhaps another three sessions before I started to realise that I was falling in love with this curious creature.

I was, at the time, only nineteen years old, so young and naïve but also at the age when you are able to fall in love without second thoughts or regrets. She was so petite and shy, so correct and neat that it was maddening.

But she also had something else: Under the surface, I believed I perceived an undercurrent of longing. Not necessarily for a lover, but maybe a yearning for a companion. Someone more like herself. Someone sensitive, who would understand the artful world from which she came and who would see into her heart and cherish her. I fervently wished that I could be that person.

*

Then came the seventh session – the one that changed everything.

I had decided that I was about to begin with the oil painting, and I had transferred one of my best sketches to a large canvas on which I had started to paint the background carefully, which had dried overnight. I was tired and restless that day and unable to do any possible constructive work until she arrived at noon as we had agreed. As usual, I made freshly brewed tea and biscuits as soon as she entered, which had become a habit.

"Did you attend the Ball yesterday?" I asked as I placed a teacup in front of her. She was wearing a perfectly ironed small and striped dark green dress today, matched by a tight jacket with numerous small pearl buttons and a short cape. *The jacket underlines her small feminine stature and enhances her waistline*, I thought sinfully.

"The Ball? No, I did not. Mr Elliott did, though," she said quietly and added, "You were there?"

"Yes, I was. However, it was dreadful. All these upper-class characters in their best gowns, enjoying each other but mostly enjoying being seen at the occasion, you know?" I grew silent, realizing that I may have offended her husband and, even worse, her own social position.

To cover it up, I blushed and decided to pour the tea. In retrospective, I can see how the accident could happen. As I clumsily filled her teacup, I shot a glance at her direction to see if she was offended, but also to steal another glance at her beautiful waist.

The distraction resulted in a disaster where I almost spilled hot tea on my most precious model, and to avoid any harm to come to her, I instead managed to pour the burning hot fluid all over my hands.

"*Mon Dieu!*" she cried out, while I echoed her lamely with a comment of my own: "Ouch!" The empty teapot hit the floor and shattered in a thousand pieces, despite the soft carpet underneath.

"Monsieur, you need to get the hands into cold water!"

"Yes, cold water," I said, slightly stunned by the increasing pain from my reddening hands. "It is in the kitchen!" I added and rose fast.

I had an old tin bucket with the water supply for the day by the fire stove, since my simple household did not have running water.

"Put them here," she said, grabbing a large soup bowl and placed both my hands into it. She then filled it with blissfully cold water. The relief was instant.

"Thank you," I said and then apologised: "I am so sorry; I am afraid I am incredibly clumsy."

"Do not be *ridicule, monsieur*! It was an accident and it could have happened to anyone."

"It feels quite much better now," I said. But as I was about to lift my hands, which were growing numb from the cold water, she seized both my hands by the wrists and pressed them back into the water.

The area where she touched my wrists burnt more than my poor fingers and placidly I obeyed. I could smell her scent, an alluring mixture of soap and dried flowers (lavender, perhaps?) as she stood next to me, almost close enough for her to touch me.

"You should keep your hands in the water for at least ten minutes. Sir," she said. Ten long strained minutes later she finally allowed me to remove my numbed hands from the bowl.

"May I?" she asked, motioning for me to put my hands in hers.

I placed my wet and dripping ungraceful fingers in her small hands, still clad in white lace gloves. She stroked my fingers and the upper side of my hands. She enquired me if it hurt and commented on the oil paint that so often decorated my fingertips. I felt hypnotised by her touch and the fact that she was so close to me.

It felt as if I was stepping into a dream as I laced my fingers with hers and drew her close, pressing her against me, and before she had time to react, I kissed her, there and then, right on the mouth. She froze for a second in my embrace, but I knew I would never let her go, not even if she had slapped me at that moment. She did a small vexing sound, and struggled against me for a second, but with a small whimper she yielded and let me kiss her.

Her attempt to struggle aroused me further and my feelings must have transferred from me to her, because within shortly, she kissed me back quite ardently, and when I started to let my hands explore her small breast through her cape, she let her hands slid in under my shirt.

After a while, she boldly started to explore my bottom, and without second thoughts, I ripped off her cape, her shirt and pulled down her petticoats to reach and kiss her small breasts.

She pulled down my breeches, and with a suppressed moan she stroked the full length of me which made me shiver and press myself against her, mumbling: "Yes, yes". I moved with her and was almost ready to come at any time.

She suddenly turned her face up, looked me directly in my eyes and said with a heavy French accent, "Please, make love to me."

I think it was the "please", or possibly the accent, or maybe her beautiful eyes, or perhaps just the combination of all of the above, which made me roughly pull away the rest of her clothes and without any hesitation enter her while she still stood half-naked in my kitchen. She was so small and petite that she weighed almost nothing, and she crossed her legs around my waist and actually let out a small snarl as I pinned her against the old kitchen wall.

At first, my pure joy and satisfaction of finally, finally merging completely made me rush the experience, but after short while, I got some sort of control over myself. I wanted this to last, and as I changed my rhythm to go slower and deeper, I paid more attention to her needs.

She had placed her hands on my hips to be able to match my pace, and as I slowed down, she closed her eyes and leaned backwards to fully enjoy the sensation. I stroked her breasts and kissed her throat as her breathing increased, and she moaned and tried to make me increase my speed. Instead, I continued with the same slow, deep and deliberate thrusts until she clawed my back, screamed out in French and finally sobbed against my shoulders.

Only then did I change my rhythm, and from her surprised hiss she had not expected me to, but as I kissed her deeply and intensely, she pinched my nipples, which made me gasp and her laugh.

My nipples have always been my sensitive spot, and as she kissed and teased me, I lost my precious control and pressed myself both faster and slightly harder against her. Her moans of pleasure made me realise that she more than appreciated this new sensation, and I gripped her around the shoulders and her hips, fully embracing her, and pushed her against me as I quickened my rhythm.

When I heard her cry out again, only then did I allow myself the full release and pleasure of lovemaking, and I came finally and utterly, almost in desperation.

For a second, I was able to stand up and carry the weight of both of us, but then my knees gave in and I slowly sank towards the stone floor, still inside of her and with her legs crossed around my back. I kissed away her tears as she cried for a while, and afterwards I held her in my arms for a long, long time.

*

The rest of the session is a blur. I remember the last frenzied minutes before the carriage arrived, helping her getting dressed, seeing her arranging her hair and stealing a few last kisses in the doorway before she reluctantly walked down to the waiting carriage.

When she was gone, I collapsed against the loveseat and with a smile remembered what we had done, still smelling her scent against my skin. Later I fell into an artistic flow and spent the rest of the afternoon and the night painting like possessed until the sun rose. The portrait was indeed astonishing; I had managed to capture the real Joan – my Joanna – not the shy little French lady, but the true essence of her being.

However, as the weeks went by, the portrait changed. The first picture was a lovely portrait of Joanna sitting on a loveseat, neat and proper. But as the sessions went by with little or no actual modelling and painting, but instead filled with activities of a more intimate character, the portrait changed. At first I thought it was an illusion, that my late-night painting and occasional glasses of wine had made me paint the alterations, but after a while it occurred to me: For every love meeting, the painting changed.

It started with a small smile on the painted Joanna's lips and a lovely blush upon her cheeks; next, her hair was in disorder; then her dress was in disarray and love bites covered her neck. It was not quite the portrait that Mr Elliott had ordered.

Not at all! And in the end I secretly gave it to her to hide, and then – for both of our sake! – I left Bath, heartbroken like only a young painter can be.

* * *

~ Wildflowers ~

"Over there! Hurry, Catherine!" Agnes cried out, trying to be heard over the summer thunder. Rain was tipping down as they ran for shelter. Just minutes ago, they had been gathering wildflowers on one of the neglected fields a couple of miles from the mansion.

Catherine's latest whim was to try to create a herbarium over the botanical species in the shire. One second the weather was fine, if perhaps a little cloudy, but such was always the weather in Exeter, close to the coast; the next second the sky had completely opened above them and was clearly on a mission to flood them all.

Agnes helped Catherine and more or less dragged her up the hill. She was worried for her friend, knowing perfectly well that Catherine's delicate health was most unsuitable for this kind of weather and that Catherine still suffered from the aftermath from a severe cold. On cue, Catherine coughed until her body shook before she gave Agnes a feeble smile.

Agnes looked up ahead of them. They had to find cover now, and she hesitated just a moment before half-carrying Catherine along. There was only one available shelter within reach.

"Is, is this really a good idea?" Catherine asked weakly as they scaled the grass-covered hill to reach the old abandoned mill. The answer was drowned out by thunderclaps.

Agnes muttered a small prayer when she found that the large entrance doors were barred, but thankfully, they were not locked. She removed the sturdy wooden bar, let it drop to the ground, put her arm around Catherine's small shivering shoulders and led her inside.

Once indoors, it took a while for them to adjust to the darkness. Occasional lighting lit up the interior through small shattered windows. The ceiling was high above them, hidden between nooks and crannies, and a small timber staircase led all the way to the top. The floor was covered with straw and old sacks of flour and grain were still stacked in a corner.

Agnes hurriedly used them to create an improvised mattress. She found also a couple of woollen horse blankets which still smelled of horses, but at least were warm and thick.

"Catherine? Cathy? I have prepared a pallet, dear."

Catherine was sitting on the floor, hugging herself closely and trying to keep warm. She only nodded in reply.

"Come. You have to get this soaked dress off and get under the blankets, or you will catch another cold."

Catherine's fingers did not obey her as she tried to unbutton the soaked walking dress. Finally Agnes had to help her undress until she was wearing only a woven cotton corset over her white linen chemise. The white underwear was nearly transparent and for the sake of decency, Catherine was quickly ushered under the blankets. Agnes wished that they had found a different refuge, preferable one with a fireplace and dry wood. She also wished for a shelter without a history of gruesome death involved.

She sat down next to Catherine and stroked the short dark curls hair away from her face. It had not grown back completely from the last time she had taken to her sick bed. Her pretty cheeks were cold as ice and she was as pale as marble. Agnes was not a little worried about her friend.

"Are you feeling better?" Agnes asked.

"C-c-cold," Catherine answered and shivered once again. Her eyes fluttered and it looked as if she was going to sleep. Or perhaps she was becoming unconscious, Agnes thought. She made a decision, and prudence be damned: Her friend was cold, and Agnes was not. She made sure that the doors were properly closed, locked them, and then she undressed quickly before she slipped in under the blankets to carefully wrap her arms around her friend's frozen body.

*

The rain was still bucketing down, the thunder getting closer. It was not a little eerie, and even though it was in the middle of the day, the mill was dark and intimidating. Agnes had heard all the stories regarding the mill and, unasked for, they came back to her.

The mill had been abandoned since the beginning of the nineteenth century when a tragic accident had occurred. According to hearsay, the mayor's young daughter, who was about to become married, had gone mad. Just a week before the wedding, she had simply disappeared. For days they had searched for her until they found her, here at the mill, swinging from the highest nook, dead to the world.

It was said that some jewellery had gone missing and that the girl had left diaries behind, crazy scribbling that was later burnt. Also, her maid vanished, never to be found, and the most frightful rumour said that the mayor's daughter had, in a fit of insanity, killed the poor girl and then committed suicide. However, another popular theory was that the maid had just seized the opportunity for some easy money and bolted. The truth had never discovered.

Nevertheless, the mill had been forsaken ever since, even though more than thirty years had passed. It was said it was haunted by the girl who never found any rest in her grave. The employees had refused to continue to work, claiming to hear crying and whispering voices at the mill, and in the end a new and more modern mill had been set up just across the Exe by the mayor before he and his family moved from the county.

Agnes shivered at her morbid thoughts and moved closer to Catherine. Thanks to the thunder, no whispering voices could be heard. Her friend felt a little bit warmer now and her breathing had slowed down. She seemed to be fast asleep, probably exhausted by the events of the day.

Agnes had always felt a certain responsibility for Catherine, even though Catherine was three years older than herself. Perhaps it was because Catherine always was a little bit lost and quite eccentric, or maybe it was because even though Catherine was a good bit taller than Agnes, she was slim as a willow branch and rather frail, the London air never quite agreeing with her.

Agnes, on the other hand, was rather petite; but the countryside life, which included long walks and riding, had shaped her body into a not so delicate female statue. Agnes gently stroked Catherine's elegant cheekbones, investigating her sleeping friend's pretty features. She fell asleep listening to Catherine's calm breathing.

*

Some time passed and the thunder seemed to have lessened some, but it could still be heard far away, and the rain was still pelting down on the slated roof of the mill. Her friend stirred, awaking slowly.

"Catherine?"

"Mmm…"

"Are you feeling any better, dear? You do not feel cold anymore, at least."

Catherine turned around, facing her and stated unexpectedly:

"I dreamt that I was getting married!"

"What? Really?" Agnes giggled. "To whom? A dark, mysterious prince? A wealthy, handsome lord? Pray tell me at once!"

Catherine tut-tutted. "As if my father would ever agree with that? Not very likely, now is it? No, it was one of those unreal dreams, and vexingly enough, I never even saw my future husband! I was running around in a large mansion filled with people I knew, but they were all acting like I was not there, and they were discussing my prospective wedding!"

"Poor dear, you must have had a fever dream! Let me see…" Agnes gently pressed her lips against her friend's forehead. It did not seem alarmingly hot.

"And then, I met you in the dream! But you were sad, hiding your face in you hands, crying and sitting all by yourself in an empty sitting room." Catherine sounded upset and miserable.

"Oh, do not fret! It was only a dream! Focus on the part where you got married instead. I like that part for sure!"

Catherine sighed.

"Well, that is not going to happen for either of us unless a miracle occurs, now is it? Old spinsters like us, we are all doomed," she added in mock self-remorse.

And it was true; neither Catherine nor Agnes could look forward to a happy marriage, or to matrimony at all to be honest. Catherine's father was completely confident that no man was good enough for his only daughter and child, while Agnes had three older sisters who were all out. For every season Catherine and Agnes continued to be unattached, she got half a year older. Perhaps, at the age of eight and twenty, she was already considered to be too old for a suitable match.

"Still, I wonder what it would be like, being committed," said Catherine.

"Yes, imagine having a darling husband, preferable a handsome one, to share your love and your bed with every night," Agnes lowered her voice for a dramatic effect and Catherine immediately engaged in the theatre.

"Yes," she said. "Fancy that! A beautiful husband to love and to kiss like this!" Catherine giggled and placed a fast and light kiss on her friend's lips.

"Ah, my dear maiden! Clearly you have never been kissed before! It is more like this, I presume," Agnes said and very, very gently pressed her lips against Catherine's. She had once seen her indiscreet sister kiss an officer at a ball and thought she knew how to copy the procedure.

Catherine pressed her lips softly against Agnes's, and in return Agnes very carefully opened her mouth a little bit more. Their tongues met for a short electrified second, before both of them withdrew hastily, scared and perhaps a little shocked of the result.

"Oh, dear, is that what it is like?"

"I do not know, honestly! I was only jesting. I am sorry, I truly am!" Agnes said, feeling that their game had taken the wrong turn.

"Do not be sorry! I... I think you were quite a remarkable kisser, much better than I would have expected."

"Oh. I see. Well, thank you."

"Of course, I myself am of course a superior kisser!"

"You are not!"

"I am too! Do you want me to prove it?" Catherine added slyly and smiled, self-assured that Agnes would never agree.

Agnes, hating to lose any kinds of games and bets, put on a brave smile. "Fine!" she said. "Prove it."

Catherine hesitated, then very gently stroked Agnes's cheek and placed a soft kiss first on her lips, then on her cheek and then back on her mouth.

Her lips felt moist and warm, and Agnes could not resist kissing her back. She felt Catherine's breath against her face and something deep down inside her stirred. It felt as if the kisses raced through her body and even made her toes tingle.

She wanted this to happen, and before she even had made up her mind regarding what may or may not be decent, she noted distractedly that she was gently stroking Catherine's neck, and she let her hands follow the beautiful line of Catherine's naked shoulders. Agnes heard Catherine gasp and she herself let out a small moan in return when Catherine started to rub Agnes's lower back and moved her body closer towards hers under the blanket.

Agnes realised that this was the moment in which they both should immediately stop what they were doing, but for some reason she just could not. Her own hands refused to do what she ordered them to and abandoned Catherine's soft shoulders to touch her small, but lovely, bosom gently through the corset. In turn, Catherine let her fingers slip under her friend's chemise and explored the naked part of Agnes thighs and bottom.

"This, this is not really happening, is it?" Agnes whispered, breathless as Catherine started to undo her corset.

"No, of course it is not," Catherine agreed, suppressing a small moan of delight as she pulled down the upper part of the linen undergarment and, very attentively and experimentally, kissed Agnes's soft round breasts. "But it feels unbelievable, nonetheless!"

Agnes leaned back, fully enjoying the sensation of Catherine's new kind of kiss. She buried her hands in her friend's hair and pressed her closer as Catherine kissed and licked her nipples.

The feeling of lust joining with need was overwhelming, and she had not experienced or enjoyed anything similar before. She felt Catherine's hand gently follow the curves of her body, down her thighs and then, lightly, through the thin fabric of the chemise, touch her between her legs. The sensation was indescribable and she felt new muscles – muscles she had not known she had – tighten inside her.

Without any sense of modesty, she struggled out off the annoying chemise which was in the way. She nudged herself closer towards Catherine, feeling almost dizzy with excitement, and she let out a small cry when Catherine's fingers persistently but gently stroked her anew between her legs.

The feeling of physical exaltation grew when she heard Catherine moan in pleasure, as she kissed and caressed Agnes's full breasts with increased intensity. And then it all melted together, the sensation of the incredible kisses, herself pushing against the wonderful fingers touching and stroking her wet and most sensual parts.

The sound of her own and Catherine's excited moaning mingled together with the distant thunder. Like a dam breaking, or a bird flying for the first time, the built-up pleasure released and crashed over her in wave after wave of complete pleasure and bliss.

The world stopped, imploded and was turned strangely topsy-turvy for a short second.

Agnes was sweaty, breathless, wet and completely and undeniable sated. She curled up like a lazy cat in the sunshine, still enjoying the last ripples of satisfaction, and lay naked against her friend's shoulder.

Catherine gleefully pointed out, "See, I told you I was the better kisser!"

Agnes agreed, but then again, she would have concurred with that the Earth was flat, England a republic and that surely pigs really could fly. She mumbled something about revenge, in a minute or so.

Love, she thought dreamingly, *was probably like wildflowers. It may often be found in the most unlikely places.*

* * *

~ The Governess ~

Under his calm surface, Ethan was silently grinding his teeth. He had just arrived to the family's residence in the remote parts of Northumberland to celebrate Christmas. This was a welcome break from the military daily routine as an officer in Her Majesty's Armed Forces and in a way it would be nice to get away from the brigade, which was stationed in Newcastle for the winter.

Or at least so he had tried to convince himself on his way in the uncomfortable horse carriage; however already during teatime, he had started to regret his decision.

There were five other persons gathered for tea in the grand and slightly over-furnitured sitting room. Ethan's father, Mr Richmond, was telling a story to Arnold, the oldest and most successful of the brothers and a true heir to their father's lucrative trade company.

Arnold stood with a delicate teacup in his large hands and listened attentively to their father. As each year went by, Arnold both acted and looked more and more like their father: Dark complexion, tall, barrel-chested and with slightly thinning hair.

Next to them Anna, Arnold's petite and shy wife, served tea and lemon tart at the table. She was supervised by Ethan's stepmother, Mrs Richmond, who with her sharp and bird-like features would spot a single mistake in an instant. Apart from the company was James, Ethan's younger brother. He was standing by the window, inspecting the snow-covered grounds outside.

What Arnold had in cleverness and logic, James lacked completely, however James had inherited all the good looks from their mother. In front of the frosty windows with a daydreaming stare, which probably was a result of several glasses of whiskey, James was a picture of the perfect, decadent dandy with golden hair spilling down his shoulders.

Indeed, James had seduced more women than what was generally tolerated, but he was to be married in June, if he managed to keep the engagement, something which Ethan secretly considered to be highly unlikely. Ethan himself was a kind of non-descriptive combination of both his parents: the shortest of his brothers, not muscular but neither stoat nor slender.

He had a lighter complexion than his father, but not as fair as his mother; more a mixture with dark, but not black hair and hazel eyes. He could not be called attractive, but he may perhaps be described as handsome, thanks to a cleft chin and rather high cheekbones, but he still remained unmarried. Even so, there were enough ladies who would prefer a uniform before pretty features, or at least so he was being told.

Ethan sighed and noticed that his three younger

half-sisters were missing. Mrs Richmond seemed to read his mind and her shrill voice called out:

"Darling, where is that governess? Should she not have brought the girls up by now?"

"I am sure they are on their way," their father replied. "However, I believe Miss Sophie fell ill yesterday."

"Ill? How very inconvenient. It is Christmas, after all," Mrs Richmond said as if the governess's illness was a personal insult.

"Yes, dear. Miss Sophie will probably be better in a couple of days. I asked if she wanted me to send for the pharmacist, but she declined. And she will not attend the Christmas dinner either."

"Send for the pharmacist? No, I do not believe that to be necessary. Perhaps the leech lady could have a look at her?"

"Do you mean old Mrs Dawson? She will not treat her, for some silly superstitious reason. You know how the Scots are…"

"Well, no harm done then. I am sure no one shall miss her company at the Christmas dinner. I, personally, do not like the idea of servants sitting at our table anyway," said Arnold.

"She is not really a servant, she is a governess!" Ethan interrupted to everyone's surprise, including his own.

"Oh, I will miss her at the table, it is always nice to rest one's eyes at something pretty," James smirked and received a stern look from Mrs Richmond.

"If you will excuse me, I need to go and unpack," said Ethan stiffly and left abruptly.

He fled the bigoted conversation, cursing in anger and taking long strides towards his room. The discussion was so typical his family: tasteless, vulgar and proud. As he went around a corner, he nearly walked straight into someone.

"Watch where you are going!" he said irritably before realizing that he had stumbled upon Miss Sophie Lakefield herself.

"Oh. I beg your pardon," he said, bowing stiffly. He tried to regain his posture and cursed his impoliteness. "It is you. Sophie. Miss Lakefield. I mean Miss Sophie."

"Sir," she said, curtseying. "You are here during the holidays, I presume?"

"Yes, indeed," he answered. As always, her odd and dissimilar eyes caught his attention. How could a person have one eye brown and green like a forest and the other blue like the sky?

He inspected her more closely and saw that she certainly did not look well; she looked paler than ever, almost transparent. Her otherwise glossy dark hair was matte and lifeless, tied back in a strict bun. While she perhaps had never been generously shaped, she now looked thin and drawn, making her black governess dress looking several sizes too large for her. Her uneven eyes seemed larger, pronounced by her small nose and lips, and the illness had painted dark circles under her eyes.

"I have heard that you have taken ill?" Ethan enquired worriedly.

"It is nothing, sir. I will probably be better in a couple of days. Thank you for asking. In fact I was on my way to my room, sir…"

Ethan felt like a complete imbecile. Here he was, delaying her to go to her room to rest while he was babbling away.

"No, of course. Do carry on," he said and added, "Let me know if there is anything I can do for you." He bowed and she curtseyed, and they went separated ways in the corridor.

*

Ethan very rarely drank, but after the disastrous dinner party later that evening, he opened his travelling pocket flask and miserably drank most of the rum before passing out only half-undressed in his bed. It had been a mistake coming back.

He woke up later by the feeling of being watched. Through the thick winter curtains he could see the waxing moon behind the frosted window glass. A small candle was lit at the table by the side of his bed. He sat up with a small cry of surprise when he realised that someone was sitting at the end of the bed.

"Miss Lakefield? Is that you?" he asked, his thoughts still unclear from rum and sleep. The woman in front of him had unkept long hair and was wearing only a white night gown.

"Yes," she said, calmly looking up. Her odd eyes gleamed from the candlelight.

"Why, why are you here?" he asked, the first question that appeared to him, and then for modesty's sake pulled up the winter quilt to cover his half-naked chest.

"I am here, Ethan, simply because I need you," she whispered.

The intimate response was not what Ethan had expected, but nonetheless he could feel certain parts of his body stir. It did not help that the nightgown which Sophie was wearing was quite thin and almost transparent in a most curious way. He pulled up his knees to hide the physical consequences of his sinful thoughts.

"Oh," he said, licking his lips unconsciously, and then it occurred to him. "Miss Lakefield. Are you feeling well? Have your condition worsened?" In honesty, he was such an idiot. How could he even imagine that she would enter a gentleman's room without extreme reasons?

"Ethan…" She leaned forward and slowly started to draw small patterns of an unknown design on the quilted bedding.

Ethan felt almost hypnotised as her fingers started to move closer towards him. The quilt was thick, but it felt like her touch burnt right through it as her fingers moved towards his thighs. What earlier had only stirred began to grow.

"Do you have feelings for me?" she asked, laying

her head to one side.

"Yes," he answered hoarsely.

He realised that he had been in love with her ever since she first arrived at the large and isolated estate. She had been a scared, alone and wide-eyed girl of barely sixteen years, far away from home.

His thoughts were shattered as her hand followed the inside of his legs until it reached its purpose. No female hands had touched him in years, and even though he occasionally met other soldiers to gain mutual temporary release, this was something else.

He wanted to say something about restraint and purity but her fingers silenced him. Instead, he drew her closer so that he could kiss her while she continued to touch him.

As she straddled him, he started to protest. It took the better part of his willpower to object, but really, as amazing as this felt, it was still incredibly wrong.

"We... I, I should not. I am sorry, Sophie. Miss Lakefield."

She replied only by kissing him deeply, her tongue exploring his, and she moved closer, pulling down the covers.

"No, really. Please," he protested as she pushed him down, not entirely gently. She was stronger than she looked and she completely ignored his protests, and instead smiled a little as she took off her nightgown.

She was stark naked underneath. The bedside

candle lit up every inch of her female body: the slim hips, the pale flesh, and the beautiful small, rounded breasts, one with a small birthmark just above the pink nipple. Ethan suddenly found it very hard to breathe or to have coherent thoughts. She bent over him, kissing him again and mumbling in his ear:

"I have waited for this for too long. We both know we want this."

Her nimble fingers had managed to undo his breeches and now she touched him without any layers of clothes between them. The feeling was intoxicating, but he still tried, feeble and almost delirious, to protest until she carefully guided him inside.

And then, when she determinedly and deliciously pushed her hips against his, it was all too late for regrets. He could do nothing but surrender as he gave up his last shreds of dignity. She was right, of course: This was exactly what he wanted and what he had dreamed about, even though he did not want to admit it, even to himself.

He succumbed to her and finally allowed himself to stroke her round breasts, kiss her pink nipples and meet her movements with thrusts of his own.

"Do you love me?" she asked, kissing his fingertips.

"Always."

"Do you need me?" She bit his ear hard enough to draw blood.

"Constantly."

"And do you want me?" She scratched his breast

with sharp nails leaving red marks while moving her hips in a methodically and tauntingly slow way.

"Desperately."

To prove to her that he really meant his last statement, he grabbed her hips pulled her against him. She let out a surprised little yelp, but adjusted her position and went back to slow, deep movements as she rode him.

She let her fingers stroke his chest, the insides of his thighs and even pinch his nipples in a not entirely gentle way. He growled with anticipation and tried to push harder against her, but he could not affect the pace at which they were moving.

She laughed at his growl, and to tease him she bent down and kissed him deeply, and then licked one of his nipples. She bit it carefully while looking up at him with her odd eyes which seemed to almost glow in the dark.

It made him gasp, and he met her eyes in a haze of burning desire. He knew what she was doing, and he gave up. For the second time he surrendered and whispered:

"Take me. Do what you want with me."

And she did. It was as if he had said the magical words. He could see her strange eyes grow large with contentment and she smiled warmly. She kissed him with renewed heat and finally moved her hips against him with an increased pace.

As she pushed her warm, sweaty body against him, he heard her breathing become more and more irregular, and then she came for the first time. With a low, animalistic cry she pushed harder against him and scratched his back until it felt raw. She licked his lips, pressed his hands to her breasts and begged him to come while she rode him harder.

Pinned down and at her mercy, Ethan had no choice; with his back arched back, he climaxed in ecstasy at the same time as she came again and squeezed her legs tightly around his waist.

They lay breathless in the candlelight afterwards. She was small enough to lie comfortably on his chest while their breathing slowed. Ethan felt nothing more than pleasure and the feeling of belonging.

There was nothing to say really, he decided as he lazily played with a strand of her long hair. What had happened had happened. They had no future together, and he had just ruined hers for all eternity.

"Thank you," she whispered and started to gather her nightgown.

"No. Miss Lakefield. Sophie. Thank you," he answered. "Perhaps we should…"

"Hush now," she interrupted him kindly. She kissed him gently. "Do not talk. Good night, sir." She cupped her hand, blew out the candle and left silently in the dark.

*

The day after, Ethan woke up and for the longest he hoped that it had all been a wicked dream – but then he saw the candle, the state of the bed and, well, certain love marks.

He looked terrible and it felt as if he had aged a decade, which was, of course, no more than he deserved. Taking liberties. Acting even worse than his youngest brother. And with the governess. With Sophie! Shame and guilt was eating him from within.

He packed his belongings, told the servants he was ill, and spent the rest of the day pacing his room restlessly. He could still smell her between the sheets. It was driving him insane. A part of him hoped that she would come later and both dreaded it and savoured it. What would he say? What could he say?

However, when she did come with soundless footsteps in the middle of the night, carrying a small candle and more beautiful than ever, words seemed unnecessary.

And in the end, how could he really resist her?

* * *

~ THE END ~

~ About the author ~

Lady T. L. Jennings writes all her stories by hand into classic journals. (The picture was taken in Bath, where Jane Austen lived between 1801–1806.)

Lady T. L. Jennings is a shy writer who loves the Victorian era and afternoon tea. She lives on the outskirts of Oxford in England, and writes Victorian erotica and romance with a dash of gothic mystique in longhand with a fountain pen.

She collects books, corsets, and lovers (all with varying levels of success).

Visit her website: www.mysecretquill.com or follow her on Facebook or Twitter for the latest news regarding writing and free stories.

Would you like to receive a notification when a new title from Lady T. L. Jennings has been released?

Visit www.mysecretquill.com and join the mailing list for notifications regarding new title releases, discounts on her books, and the exclusive opportunity to receive review copies of Lady T. L. Jennings books before they are published anywhere else.

~ About the stories ~

My stories have sometimes been influenced by Victorian and historical novels, for example by authors such as Charlotte Brontë, Oscar Wilde, and Jane Austen, but also the Brothers Grimm and old folk tales and modern authors e.g. Sarah Waters (Tipping the velvet), Belinda Starling (The Journal of Dora Damage), and Susanna Clarke (Jonathan Strange & Mr Norrell).

Sometimes it is a specific place that inspires an idea to my stories. I wrote "View of a Cemetery" after I had visited Highgate Cemetery in London and I have also been to Bath where "The portrait of Mrs Elliott" is set.

For all of my stories I try to do as much research as possible (mostly because I am quite fond of reading about the Victorian era, but also because I like to write accurate historical stories). For the short stories in this collection I researched all kind of things including: British hunting traditions and seasons, the Great Expedition in Hyde Park, Victorian fashion and etiquette, and smaller details such as the introduction of gas street lighting in London.

The footnotes in the Penguin Classic editions of their Victorian novels have also helped me further.

* * *

*I hope you enjoyed reading this story
as much as I liked writing it!*

My Secret Quill